THE GIRL IN GRAY

A May Iverson Story

Elizabeth Jordan

first published in

1914

Nine typewriters were stuttering over nine news stories; four electric fans were singing their siren songs of coolness; two telephone bells were ringing; one office boy, new to his job, was hurtling through the air on his way to the night city editor's desk, and the night city editor was discharging him because he was not coming faster; the managing editor was “calling down” a copy-reader; the editor-in-chief was telling the foreign editor he wished he could find an intelligent man to take the foreign desk; Mr. Nestor Hurd was swearing at Mr. Godfrey Morris. In other words, it was nearly midnight in the offices of the *Searchlight*.

I was sitting at my desk, feeling very low in my mind. That day, for the first time in my three weeks' experience as a reporter, Mr. Hurd had not given me an assignment. This was neither his fault nor mine. I had written a dozen good stories for him, besides many more that were at least up to the average. My assignments had taken me to all sorts of places strangely unlike the convent from which I had graduated only a month before--morgues, hospitals, police stations, the Tombs, the Chinese quarter--and I had always brought back something, even, as

Mr. Gibson had once muttered, if it were merely a few typhoid germs. Mr. Gibson did not approve of sending me to all those places. Only that morning I had heard my chief tell Mr. Morris the Iverson kid was holding down her job so hard that the job was yelling for help. This was a compliment, for Mr. Hurd never joked about any one who worked less than eighteen hours a day.

I knew he hated to see me idle now, even for a few hours, and I did not like it myself. But we both had to bear it, for this had been one of the July days when nothing happened in New York. Individuals were born, and married, and died, and were run over by automobiles, as usual; but, as Mr. Hurd said, “the element of human interest was lacking.” At such times the newspapers fill their space with symposiums on “Can a Couple Live on Eight Dollars a Week?” or “Is Suicide a Sin?” Or they have a moral spasm over some play and send the police to suppress it. The night before Mr. Hurd had sent Gibson, his star reporter, with a police inspector, to see a play he hoped the *Searchlight* could have a moral spasm over. Mr. Gibson reported that the police inspector had left the theater wiping his eyes and saying he meant to look after his daughters better hereafter; so the *Searchlight* could not have a spasm that time, and Mr. Hurd swore for five minutes without repeating once. He was wonderful that way, but not so gifted as Col. John Cartwell, the editor-in-chief, who used to check himself between the syllables of his words to drop little oaths in. Such conversation was new and terrible to me. I had never heard any one swear before, and at first it deeply offended me. I thought a convent girl should not hear such things, especially a girl who intended to be a nun when she was twenty-one. But after a week or two I discovered that the editors never meant anything by their rude words; they were merely part of their breath.

To kill time that evening I wrote a letter to my mother--the first long one I had sent her since I left my Western home. I wrote it on one side of my copy paper, underlining my "u's" and overlining my "n's," and putting little circles around all my periods, to show the family I was a real newspaper woman at last. When I finished the letter I put it in an office envelope with a picture of the *Searchlight* building on the outside, and began to think of going home. But I did not feel happy. I realized by this time that in newspaper work what one did yesterday does not matter at all; it is what one does to-day that counts. In the convent we could bask for a fortnight in the afterglow of a good recitation, and the memory of a brilliant essay would abide, as it were, for months. But full well I knew that if I gave Mr. Hurd the biggest "story" of the week on Thursday, and did nothing on Friday, he would go to bed Friday night with hurt, grieved feelings in his heart. This was Friday.

However, there was no sense in waiting round the office any longer, so I put on my hat and left the *Searchlight* building, walking across City Hall

Park to Broadway, where I took an open car up-town. I was getting used to being out alone late at night; but I had not ceased to feel an exultant thrill whenever I realized that I, May Iverson, just out of the convent and only eighteen, was actually part of the night life of great, wonderful, mysterious New York. Almost every man and woman I saw interested me because of the story I knew was hidden in each human heart; so to-night, as usual, I studied closely those around me. But my three fellow-passengers did not look as if they had any stories in them. They were merely tired, sleepy, perspiring men going home after a day of hard work. I envied them. I had not done a day's work, and I felt that I hardly deserved to rest. This thought was still in my mind when I left the car at Twenty-fifth Street and walked across Madison Square toward the house where I had rooms.

It was after midnight and very hot. The benches in the park still held many men--most of them the kind that stay there because they have no place else to go. There were a dozen tramps, some stretched at full length and sound asleep, others talking together. There were men out of work, trying to read the newspaper advertisements by the electric light from the globes far above them. Over the park hung a yellow mist that looked like fog but was merely heat, and from every side came the deep mutter of a great city on a summer night. The men around me were the types I had seen every time I crossed the Square, and, though I was always sorry for them, they no longer made me feel sick with sympathy, as they did at first.

But on a bench a little apart from the rest sat a girl who interested me at once. I noticed her first because she was young and alone, and then because she seemed to be in trouble. She was drooping forward in her seat, with her elbows on her knees and her chin in her hands, staring hard at a spot on the ground in front of her. I could not see what it was. It looked like an ordinary brown stain. I usually walked very fast when I was alone at night, but now I slackened my pace and strolled toward the girl as slowly as I dared, studying her as I went. I could not see much of her face, which was in the hollow of her joined hands, but the way she was sitting--all bunched up--showed me that she was sick or discouraged, or both. She wore a gray dress with a very narrow skirt, and a wide, plain lace collar on the jacket. The suit had a discouraged air, as if it had started out to be smart and knew it had failed. Her hat was a cheap straw with a quill on it that had once been stiff but was now limp as an unstarched collar, and the coil of hair under it was neat and brown and wavy. Her plain lingerie blouse was cut low at the neck and fastened with a big black bow, and when I was closer to her I saw that both her shoes were broken at the sides. Altogether, she looked very sick and very poor, and when she changed her position a little to glance at a man who was passing, something about her profile made me think of one of my classmates at St.

Catharine's.

I had tried to pass her, but now my feet would not take me. It was simply impossible to ignore a girl who looked like Janet Trelawney and who seemed to be in trouble. I saw when I got nearer that she was not Janet, but she might have been--and, anyway, she was a young girl like myself. We were taught at the convent that to intrude on another person's grief, uninvited, is worse than to intrude at any other time. Mere sympathy does not excuse it. But this looked like a special case, for there was no one else around to do anything for the girl in gray if she needed help.

However, I did not speak to her at once. I merely sat down on the bench beside her and waited to see if she would speak to me.

She raised her head the minute she felt me there, and sat up and stared at me with eyes that were big and dark and had a queer, desperate expression in them.

It seemed to startle her to know that some one was so near her, but after she had looked at me her surprise changed to annoyance, and she moved as if she meant to get up and go away. That full glance at her had shown me what she was like. She was not pretty. Her face was dreadfully pale, her nose was ordinary in shape, and her firmly set, thin lips made her mouth look like a straight line. I did not see how I could have thought of Janet Trelawney in connection with her. However, I felt that I could not drive her away from her seat, so I stopped her and begged her pardon and asked if she was ill or had hurt herself in any way, and if I could help her.

At first she did not answer me. She merely sat still and looked me over slowly, as if she were trying to make up her mind about me. The longer she looked the more puzzled she seemed to be. It had been raining when I left home in the morning, so I had on a mackintosh and a little soft rainy-day hat. I knew I did not look impressive, and it was plain that the girl in gray did not think much of me. At last she asked what I wanted, and her voice sounded hard and indifferent--even rude. I was disappointed in that, too, as well as in her face. It would have been more interesting, of course, to help a refined, educated girl. There was no doubt, however, that she needed help of some kind, so I merely repeated in different words what I had said to her at first. She laughed then--a laugh I did not like at all--and stared at me again in her queer way, as if she could not make me out. She seemed to be more puzzled over me than I was over her.

She kept on staring at me a long time with her singular eyes, that had dark circles under them. At last she asked me if I was a "society agent" or anything of that sort, and when I said I was not she asked how I happened to be out so late, and what I was doing. Her voice was as queer as her eyes--low and husky. I did not like her manner. It almost seemed as if she thought I had no right to be there, so I told her rather coldly that I was a reporter on the *Searchlight* and that I was on my way home from the office. As soon as I said that her whole manner changed. I have noticed this quick change in others when they hear that I am a newspaper woman. Some are pleased and some are not, but few remain cold and detached. The girl in gray actually looked relieved about something. She laughed again, a husky, throaty laugh that sounded, however, much nicer and more human than before, and gave me a good-natured little push.

"Oh," she said, "all right. Better beat it now. So-long." And she waved me away as if she owned the park bench. I hesitated. I was sorry now that I had stopped, and I wanted to go; but it seemed impossible to leave her there. I sat still for a moment, thinking it over, and suddenly she leaned toward me and advised me very earnestly not to linger till the roundsman came to take my pedigree. She said he was letting her alone because he knew she was only out of the hospital two days and up against it, but the healthy thing for me was to move on while the walking was good.

I was sorry she used so much slang, but of course the fact that she was unrefined and uneducated made her situation harder, and demanded even more sympathy from those better off. What she had said about the hospital and being "up against it" proved that I had done right to stop.

I told her I was going home in a few minutes, but that I wanted to talk to her first if she did not mind, and that there was no reason why I could not sit in the park if she could. She looked at me and laughed again as if I had made a joke, and the laugh brought on an attack of coughing which kept her busy for a full minute. When she had stopped I pointed out my home to her. It was on the opposite side of the Square, but we could see it quite plainly from where we sat. We could even see the windows of my rooms, which faced the park. The girl in gray looked up at them a long time.

"Gee!" she said, "you're lucky. Think of havin' a joint to fall into, and not knowin' enough to go to it when you got a chance." She added, "It wouldn't take me long to hop there if I owned the latch-key."

I asked her where she lived, and she

laughed again and swung one knee over the other as we were taught in the convent not to do, and muttered that her present address was Madison Square Park, but she hoped it would not be permanent. Then she got up and said, "So-long," and started to go. I got up, too, and caught her arm. Her last words had simply thrilled me. I had read about girls being sick and out of work and being dismissed from the hospital with no money and no place to go to. But to read of them in books is one thing, and to see one with your own eyes, to have one actually beside you, is another thing--and very different. My heart swelled till it hurt; so did my throat. The girl shook off my hand.

“Say,” she said, and her voice was rude and cross again--”say, kid, what’s the matter with you? You ain’t got nothin’ on me. Beat it, will you, or let me beat it. I can’t set here and chin.”

I held her arm. I knew what was the matter.

She was too proud to ask for help. I knew another thing, too. There was a story in her, the story of what happens to the penniless girl in New York; and I could get it from her and write it and put the matter on a business basis that would mean as much to her as to me. Then I would have my story, the story I had not got to-day, and she would have a room and shelter, for of course I would give her some money in advance. My mind worked like lightning. I saw exactly how the thing could be done.

"Wait a minute," I said. "Forgive me--but you're hungry, aren't you?"

She stared at me again with that

queer look of hers. Then she answered with simple truth. "You bet I am," she muttered.

"Very well," I said, and I put all the will-power I had in my voice. "Come with me and get something to eat. Then tell me what has happened to you. Perhaps I can make a newspaper story of it. If I can, we'll divide the space rates."

The girl in gray hung back. I could see that she wanted to go with me, but that for some reason she was afraid.

"Say," she said at last, "you're kidding ain't you? You don't look like a reporter nor act like one. Honest, you got me guessin'."

I did not like that very much, but I could not blame her. I knew it required more than three weeks to make one look like a real newspaper woman. I opened my hand-bag and took out one of the new cards I had had engraved, with *The New York Searchlight* down in the left-hand corner. It looked beautiful. I could see that at last the girl in gray was impressed. She stood with the card in her hand, staring down at it and thinking. Finally she shrugged her shoulders and clapped me on the back with a force that hurt me.

"Al-l-l *right!*" she said, drawling out the first word and shooting the second at me like a bullet from a pistol. "I got the goods. I'm just out of Bellevue. I'll give you a spiel about the way those guys treated me. I'll tell you about the House of Detention, too, and the judges and the police. Oh, I got a story, all right, all right. I'll give it to you straight."

She was pulling me

along the street as she talked. She seemed to be in a great hurry all of a sudden, and in good spirits, but I realized how weak she was when I saw that even to walk half a block made her breath come in little gasps.

“It’s the eats first, ain’t it?” she asked; and I told her it certainly was. Then

I asked her where we were going, for it was clear that she was headed for some definite place.

"Owl-wagon," she told me, and saved her breath for the walk. I said we would take a car, but she pointed to the "owl-wagon" standing against the curb only a square away. The sight of it seemed to give her fresh strength. She made for it like a carrier-pigeon going home. When we reached it she sat down on the curbstone and nodded affably to the man inside the wagon. He nodded back at her and then came through the door and down the wagon steps to stare at me.

"Hello," he said to the girl in gray. "Heard you was sick. Glad to see you round again. What'll you eat?"

She did not waste breath on him, but made a gesture toward me. For a moment I think she could not speak.

"Give her a large glass of milk first," I told the man--"not too cold." When I handed it to her I advised her to drink it slowly, but she did not. It vanished in one long gulp. While the man was filling another glass for her I asked her what she wanted for supper. Eating at the "owl" was a new experience to me. I began to enjoy it, and to examine the different kinds of food that stood on the little shelves around the sides of the wagon. The girl in gray looked at me over the rim of her glass.

"What'll you stand for?" she asked.

I laughed and told her to choose for herself; she could have everything in the wagon if she wanted it. Before the words were past my lips she was on the top step, selecting sandwiches and pie and ordering the man around as if she owned the outfit. She took three sandwiches, one of every kind he had, and two pieces of pie, and some doughnuts. When she had all she wanted she got down from the wagon and backed carefully to the curb, balancing the food in her hands. Then she sat down again and smiled at me for the first time. Something about that smile made me want to cry; but she seemed almost happy.

“Ain’t this a bit of all right?” she asked, with her mouth full. She told the proprietor that his pies had less sawdust in them than last year and that he must have put some real lemon in one of them by mistake. While they talked I continued to inspect the inside of the wagon, but I heard the owl-man ask her a question in a whisper that must have reached across the street. "Say,

Mollie, who's your friend?" he wanted to know.

The girl in gray told him it was none of his business. Her speech sounded strangely like that of Mr. Hurd. There were several of his favorite words in it. I sighed. She was a dreadfully disappointing girl, but she had been starving, and I had only to look at her face and her poor torn shoes to feel sympathy surge up in me again. When she was finishing her last piece of pie she beckoned to me to come and sit beside her on the curb.

"Now for the spiel," she said, and her husky voice sounded actually gay. "You got the key. Wind me up. I'll run 's long's I can."

I looked around. The street was deserted except for two men who stood beside the owl-wagon munching sandwiches. They stared hard at us, but did not come near us. There was a light in the wagon, too, by which I might have made some notes. But I did not want to get my story at one o'clock in the morning out on a public avenue. I wanted a room and a reading-lamp and chairs and a table. Six months later I could write any story on the side of a steam-engine while the engine was in motion, but this was not then. Besides, while the girl was eating I had

had an inspiration. I asked her if she had really meant what she said about having no place to go but the park; and when she answered that she had, I asked her where she would have gone that night if I had not come along. She looked at me, hesitated a moment, and then turned sulky.

"Aw, what's the use?" she said. "Get busy. Do I give you the story, or don't I?"

I told her she did. Then I produced my inspiration. "Aren't there homes for the friendless," I asked her, "where girls are taken in for a night when they have no money?"

The girl in gray said there were, and sat

eyeing me with her lower jaw lax and a weary, discouraged air.

"All right," I said, briskly; "let's go to one."

It took her a long time to understand what I meant. I had to explain over and over that I wanted to go with her and see exactly how girls were received and treated in such places and what sort of rooms and food they got, and that I must play the part of a penniless and friendless girl myself to get the facts; for of course if the people in the "refuge" knew I was a reporter everything would be colored for me. At last my companion seemed to grasp my meaning.

She got up, wabbling a little on her weak knees, and started toward Twenty-third Street.

"Come on, then," she muttered, and added something about a "funeral" and some one being "crazy." She said the place we were going to was on First Avenue, not very far away, but I stopped a car and made her get into it. As we rode across town she told me the little she knew about the refuge. She said girls who went there paid a few cents for their rooms if they had money, but if not they were sometimes taken in without charge. She said breakfast was five cents and dinner ten or more, according to what one ate.

The house closed at midnight, and she was afraid we could not get in; but she had been there twice before, and the matron knew she was sick, so perhaps she would admit us. I was to be Kittie Smith, a friend of hers from Denver.

I did not like the appearance of the place very much

when we finally reached it. It was like a prison, I thought, and its black windows seemed to glower at us menacingly as we looked at them. We climbed the worn steps that led to the front door; there were only a few of them, but I had to help the girl in gray. When we reached the last one, she rang the bell labeled

“Night bell.” Beside it a brass sign that needed polishing told us the institution was a “Home for Friendless Girls.” We could hear the bell jangling feebly far inside the house, as if it hung at the end of a loose wire, but for a long time no one answered it. The girl in gray sat down on the top step while I rang the bell again.

Then at last steps came along the hall, the door opened an inch, and an old woman peered out at us. We could see nothing of her but her eyes and a bit of white hair. The eyes looked very cross, and the old woman's voice matched them when she spoke to us. She asked what we wanted and explained in the same breath that the house was closed and that it was too late to get in. The girl in gray leaned back against the door so the old woman could not close it, and said in a faint voice that she was sick.

"You remember me, Mrs. Catlin," she added, coaxingly. "Sure you do. I'm Mollie Clark. I been here before."

Mrs. Catlin opened the door another inch, grudgingly, and surveyed Mollie Clark.

"Humph!" she said. "It's you again, is it?"

She hesitated a moment and again looked Mollie Clark over. Then she flung the door wide without a word and let us into a long hall with a bare floor, whitewashed walls, and a flight of stairs at the end of it. A gas-light, turned very low, burned at the rear, and the whole house smelled of carbolic acid. It seemed to me that no girl's situation anywhere could be as forlorn as that place looked. The old woman picked up a candle which stood on a table near the door and lit it at the solitary gas-jet. Then she motioned to us to follow her and started rheumatically up-stairs, grumbling under her breath all the way. She said it was against the rules to let us in at that hour, and she didn't know what the superintendent would say in the morning, and that there was only one room empty, anyhow, and we would have to be content with it. She led us up three flights of stairs and into a little hall-room at the front of the house. It had one window, which was open. Its furniture was a small bed, a wash-stand with a white bowl and pitcher, one towel, a table, and two chairs. My eyes must have lit up when they saw the table. That was what I wanted, and I did not care much about anything else.

Mrs. Catlin set the candle down on the table, whispered something about taking our “records” in the morning, warned us not to talk and disturb others, and went away without saying good night. The minute the door closed behind her I sat down at the table and got out my pencil and a fat note-book. I did not even stop to take off my hat, but Mollie Clark removed hers and threw it in a corner. Her hair, as I had suspected, was very pretty--soft and brown and wavy. She came and sat down opposite me at the table and waited for me to begin.

At first when we got into the room I had felt rather queer--almost nervous. But the minute I had my pencil in my hand and saw my note-book open before me I forgot the place we were in and was comfortable and happy. I smiled at Mollie Clark and told her to tell me all about herself--the whole story of her life, so that I could use as much or as little of it as I wanted to. Of course, she did not know how to begin. People never do. She rested her elbows on the table and her chin on her hands, which seemed to be her favorite attitude, and sat quite still, thinking.

To help her I asked a few questions. That started her, and at last she grew interested and more at ease and began to talk.

I will admit right here that before fifteen minutes had passed I was in an abyss of black despair. Someway I simply could not get hold of that story, and when I did begin to get hold of it I was frightened. It was not because she used so much slang. I understood that, or most of it. But some of the things she said I did not understand at all, and when I showed I did not, or asked her what they meant, she was not able to explain them. She put them in a different way, but I did not get them that way, either; and she looked so surprised at first, and so discouraged herself toward the end, that at last I stopped asking her questions and simply wrote down what she told me, whether I knew what it meant or not. After a time I began to feel as if some one in a strange world was talking to me in an unknown tongue--which little by little I began to comprehend. It seemed a horrible sort of world, and the words suggested unspeakable things. Once or twice I felt sick and giddy--as if something awful was coming toward me in a dark room and would soon take hold of me. Occasionally the girl leaned across the table to look at my notes and see what I was putting down, and I kept pushing my chair farther and farther away from her. I hoped it would not hurt her feelings, but I could not endure her near me.

For five minutes the story went beautifully. She had run away from home when she was only sixteen--three years before; and the home had been a farm, just as it is in books. She had gone to Denver--the farm was thirty miles from Denver, but not large enough to be a ranch--and she had worked for a while in a big shop and afterward in an office. She had never learned typewriting or shorthand or expert filing, nor anything of that kind, so she folded circulars and addressed envelopes, and got five dollars a week for doing it. She said it was impossible to live on five dollars a week, and that this was the beginning of all her trouble.

After that she

talked about her life in Chicago and Detroit and Buffalo and Boston and New York, and about men who had helped her and women who had robbed her, and police graft, and a great many things I had never even heard of.

For a long time I wrote as fast as my hand could write. My head seemed to be spinning round on my shoulders. I felt queerer and queerer, and more and more certain I was in a nightmare; the worst part of the nightmare was the steady husky whisper of the girl's voice--for of course she had to whisper. At moments it seemed like the hissing of a snake, and the girl looked like a snake, too, with her set straight mouth and her strange, brilliant eyes. At last, after a long time, I stopped writing and leaned back in my chair and looked at her. At the same time she stopped talking and looked back at me, and for a minute neither of us spoke. Then she bunched forward in her chair and sat staring at the floor, exactly the way she had done in the park.

“It’s no go,” she said, in a queer, flat voice. “You ain’t gettin’ it, are you?”

For a moment I did not answer her. It seemed someway that I could not. I saw by her face how she felt--sick with disappointment. She muttered some words to herself. They sounded like unpleasant words; I was glad I did not hear them clearly. She had counted on her share of the space rates for my story. She sat still for quite a long time. Once or twice she looked at me as if she did not understand why I was allowed to encumber the earth when I was so stupid. Then she shrugged her shoulders, and finally she smiled at me in a sick kind of way. I suppose she remembered that, after all, I had given her a supper. At last she rose and picked up her hat and put it on.

"I'll blow out of here," she said. "Sorry you're out a

meal for nothin'."

She turned to go, and I felt more emotions in that moment than I had ever felt before. There were dozens of them, but confusion and horror and pity seemed to be the principal ones. I asked her to wait a minute, and I went to my hand-bag and took out my purse. There was not very much in it. I had been paid on Saturday, and this was Friday, so of course I had spent most of my money. But there were six dollars left, and I gave her five of them.

"What for?" she asked, and stared at me as she had done in the park.

"For the story," I said. "On account.

I'll give you the rest when it's printed."

She took the bill and stood still, looking down at it as it lay in her hand. Then suddenly she threw it on the floor.

"Aw, say," she muttered, "what's the use? It's like takin' candy from a kid. You'll need that money," she added, touching the bill with the toe of her ragged shoe as she spoke. “You’ll sure need it to get back where you come from. You didn’t get that story. You didn’t get a word of it.”

The look of the ragged shoe as she put it out and pushed the money away, and the look on her face as she spoke, made my heart turn over with pity for her. I picked up my note-book and held it toward her.

"Didn't I get it?" I asked. "Look at this."

She took the note-book and turned the pages, at first slowly and without hope, then with interest. Finally, without raising her eyes, she sat down by the flickering candle and read them all. While she read I watched her, and as I looked I realized that there was another Watcher in the little room with us--one who stood close beside her, waiting, and who would wait only a few weeks. I knew now what her cough meant, and her husky voice, and the stain in the park, and the red spots that came and went on her thin cheeks.

When she had finished reading the notes she laid down the book and smiled at me. “Kiddin’ me again, wasn’t you?” she said, quietly. “You got it all here, ain’t you?”

“Yes,” I said. “I’ve got the story.”

“Sure you have,” she corroborated. “That

Bellevue stuff's great. And take it from me, your editor will eat up the story about Holohan, with the names an' the dates an' the places. Here's six girls will swear to what I told you. And Miss Bates, the probation officer, she'll stand for it, too. I'd have give it to a paper long ago if I'd known who to go to."

An attack of coughing stopped her words. After it she leaned against the table for a moment, exhausted. Then she bent and picked up the bill from the floor. Last of all she took my pencil out of my hand, wrote a name and address in my note-book, and laid the book back on the table.

"Me for the outer darkness," she said. "That's where I'll be. I'll stay in till four to-morrow afternoon, if your editor wants anything else."

She hesitated a moment, as if struggling with words that wouldn't come. "Thanks for the banquet," she got out, at last. "So-long."

I looked straight into her strange eyes. There were many things I wanted to say to her, but I didn't know how. I felt younger than I had ever felt before, and ignorant and tongue-tied.

"You stay here," I said. "I'll go home."

The girl's eyes looked big and round as she stared at me.

She held up the five-dollar bill in her hand.

“Stay here,” she gasped, “when I got money to go somewhere else? D’ye think I’m crazy? You got to stay an’ get the rest of yer story. I ain’t! See?”

I saw.

“You’ll go right to that address,” I asked, “and rest?”

"Sure I will," she told me, cheerfully.

"I'll bring your half of the money to you as soon as I get it," I ended. "Probably in two or three days. And I'm going to send a doctor to see you to-morrow."

She was on her way to the door as I spoke, but she stopped and looked back at me. "Say, kid," she said, "take my advice. Don't bring the money. *Send* it. Get me?"

I nodded. The door closed very softly behind her. I heard the old stairs creak once or twice as she crept down them. Then I went to the open window and leaned out. She was leaving the house, and I watched her until she turned into a side street. She walked very slowly, looking to the right and to the left and behind her, as if she felt afraid.

Two mornings later when I entered the city room of the *Searchlight* Mr. Gibson rose and bowed low before me. Then he backed away, still bowing, and beckoning to me at the same time. His actions were mysterious, but I followed him across the room, and several reporters rose from their desks and followed us both. Near the city editor's desk Mr. Gibson stopped, made another salaam, and pointed impressively to the wall. Tacked on it very conspicuously was a “model story” of the day--the sort of thing the city editor occasionally clipped from the Searchlight or some other newspaper and hung there as “an inspiration to the staff.” We were always interested in his “model stories,” for they were always good; I had read some of them till I knew them by heart. But this particular morning it was my story which was tacked there--my story of the girl in gray!

For a full minute I could not speak. I merely stood and stared while the reporters congratulated me and joked around me. While I was still trying to take in the stupendous fact that the "model story of the day" was really mine the city editor, Mr. Farrell, came and stood beside me. He was a fat man, with a face like a sad full moon, but he was smiling now.

"Nice story," he said, kindly. "But don't get a swelled head over it. You'll probably write a rotten one to-morrow."

I nodded. Full well I knew I probably would.

"Besides," continued Mr. Farrell, "the best thing in your story was the tip it gave us for Gibson's big beat. That was a cub reporter's luck. Thanks to it, we've got Holohan with the goods on. If you listen you'll hear him squeal. And oh, by the way," he added, as he was turning back to his desk, "we have a dozen messages already from people who want to give care and nursing and country homes to your 'girl in gray.'"

I was glad of that. Also I was interested in something else, and I mentioned it to Mr. Farrell. I told him I had felt sure my story was spoiled because I had left so much out of it. The city editor looked at me, and then jerked his head toward the story on the wall.

"It's what you left out of it," he said, "that makes that a model story."

ABOUT THE AUTHOR

Elizabeth Jordan was an American journalist, author, editor, and suffragist. Often remembered for her early support of Sinclair Lewis, and her relationship with Henry James, she was a significant author in her own right and the editor of *Harper's Baazar* from 1900 to 1913.

ABOUT THE COVER

The image on the cover is adapted from a photograph of typewriter in Santiago, Chile taken by McKay Savage.

MAY IVERSON RETURNS IN *IN GAY BOHEMIA*

MORE BOOKS AT:

superlargeprint.com

KEEP ON READING!

The cover is adapted from a photo by McKay Savage (CC BY 2.0)
This book is set in a font designed by Abelardo Gonzalez called OpenDyslexic

ISBN 9781072851080

Made in the USA
Coppell, TX
03 December 2020